OCT 1979
RECEIVED
OHIO DOMINICAN
COLLEGE LIBRARY
COLUMBUS, OHIO
43219

THE STORY ON THE
WILLOW PLATE

THE WILLOW DESIGN

THE STORY ON THE

Willow Plate

ADAPTED FROM THE
CHINESE LEGEND BY

LESLIE THOMAS

WITH ILLUSTRATIONS
BY THE AUTHOR

NEW YORK ○ ○ ○ 1940
WILLIAM MORROW AND COMPANY

J
398.2
T

THE STORY ON THE
WILLOW PLATE

Copyright - - 1940
BY LESLIE THOMAS

PRINTED IN THE UNITED STATES
BY QUINN & BODEN COMPANY, INC.,
RAHWAY, N. J.

for

CEDRIC AND BRAD

108689

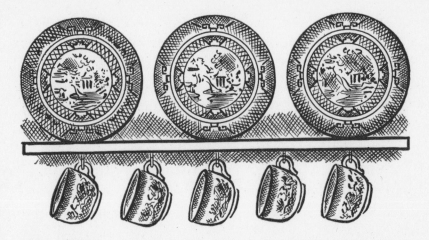

HERE is a story that most of us have right in our own cupboards. It is written in pictures on the plates and on the cups and saucers. The design on these plates is called the Willow Pattern and it has been a familiar decoration on our tables for many years.

No one seems to know who originated the design or the story that it tells. It first appeared in England at about the time when George Washington was President of the United States. More than likely it was copied from an old plate brought from China.

Even in those days China was a great nation. It

was a land of fine artists and skillful craftsmen who made beautiful carvings in stone and jade. They painted pictures with delicate skill and produced objects of unsurpassed beauty in porcelain—plates and cups as fragile as eggshells, and decorated with symbolic designs such as the Willow Pattern.

The Willow Pattern is so called because of the willow tree which you can see if you study the plate. It is near the little bridge on which are three figures. These little people are running toward a house near the other end of the bridge. It is a poor little house set on uncultivated land, represented by wavy lines beneath it. Above it is a fir tree, which is a poor tree, bearing no fruit.

In contrast to this poor house is the house on the other side of the plate. It has two stories, which show us that the owner is very wealthy. It is the home of a great lord—a mandarin. The lands surrounding it are well tilled and bear a rich crop. The orange and lemon trees are heavily laden with fruit, and the air is perfumed with jasmine and mimosa. At one side is a peach tree in full bloom. To the right of the great house and above the trees can be seen a sum-

THE MANDARIN'S HOUSE

mer house. To the left is a little addition—a pavilion which juts out into the water. There is a terrace beneath the pavilion where people could walk in the quiet evening and watch the ripples on the river.

A pathway runs from the steps of the house to the bottom of the design. Stretching from the side of the estate to the water's edge is a wooden wall which cuts directly across the path.

Higher up on the design is a boat with a house on its deck and a little figure standing in the bow. The boat is drifting along the river toward another estate. This house is not as large as the great house

of the mandarin but it is better than the poor little
house near the bridge. The ground around it is well
cultivated, as you can see by the lumpy soil which
the artist has drawn. Even where the banks jut out
into the river, they are tilled to the water line. The
house is set in an orchard of orange, lemon and per-
simmon trees. If you look closely you will see smoke
and flames rising from the roof of the house to the
edge of the design.

THE SUMMER HOUSE

Now you see all the picture. There is the mandarin's house and the wooden wall which cuts across the pathway. The flowering peach tree is there, and the willow, the bridge and the poor little house with the figures running toward it. What have the river and the boat to do with the story—and the fine little estate, so carefully cultivated? And the fire! What is the story this picture tells?

Surely, our plate must hold an interesting tale. Perhaps it will tell us about the two doves, at the top of the design, that fly toward each other to kiss.

Listen, and the whole picture will come to life. No longer blue spots on a china plate, it will become real people and houses and trees. The boatman will guide his craft between the rocks in a rain-swollen river. You will hear a legend of old China that has lived with us in our homes for these many years, hidden away among the cups and saucers in the cupboard.

T'SO LING

MANY years ago there lived in China a mandarin named T'so Ling. He dwelt in a great marble house on the bank of a river. His richly embroidered robes were made of the finest silks and he ate from dishes so delicate that light showed through them. His chopsticks were of gold and ivory, and the nail of his little finger was eight inches long and was protected by a sheath of pure gold. He was proud of the length of this fingernail, for it showed that he was a great lord who never had to work with his hands.

T'so Ling's garden was filled with beautiful flowers and sweet-smelling herbs. In his fruit-laden trees golden-voiced song birds built their nests. His house was filled with costly tapestries and rare jades, and the fragrant smoke of incense brought from far places was wafted through the spacious rooms.

Perhaps the mandarin's greatest treasure was his little daughter, Koong-se, who was more beautiful than the moon and the stars. Each day Koong-se sat in the summer house in the garden and played with her pet nightingale. Sometimes she played with her ivory spool and sticks. She would throw the spool high into the air and catch it on a silken cord tied between the two sticks, balance it there and throw it into the air again.

Wherever she went she was followed by her faithful nurse, Chun Soy, who knew her every secret. Koong-se was happy in the jasmine-scented garden. Chun Soy knew that she was happy because she was in love.

Now among T'so Ling's many servants was a youth named Chang, who acted as his secretary. Chang was a clever young man. He performed his duties for the mandarin well, but hoped some day to become a great poet.

Each day when Chang's work was done he would hasten to the summer house. Each day when the lotus bloom folded its petals he found Koong-se waiting for him.

As the lovers sat in the summer house, building castles in the air, the faithful Chun Soy watched at the pathway, fearful of the old mandarin's approach. And Chang read his newest poem to little Koong-se. One evening the lovers sat there and the nightingale sang to them from his golden cage. Chun Soy sat

KOONG-SE

outside and listened to its song as she watched the pathway. The warm breeze and the voice of the little bird made her close her eyes. Soon she was asleep. Koong-se and Chang sat side by side in the summer house and looked lovingly at each other while the nightingale sang.

Suddenly they were startled by the angry voice of the mandarin who had come along the path unseen by the drowsy Chun Soy.

"What means this?" he thundered, glaring at Chang. "Begone, knave," he cried. "Leave this house—and a thousand curses on your miserable head!"

Poor Chang, knowing well that his case was hopeless, left in humiliation. He knew that a poor servant never should have courted the daughter of the rich mandarin. As for little Koong-se—she wept bitterly as her angry father marched her into the house to be locked in her room.

Chun Soy, the faithful nurse, was dismissed and her place given to a watchful old woman whose heart was as shriveled as her ugly face. The mandarin, fearing that Chang might come back and attempt

CHANG

THE OLD HAG

to see his daughter, caused a high wooden wall to be built across the estate to the water's edge. He also built a pavilion adjoining the house in which to imprison the unhappy Koong-se. This new building jutted out into the river and had terraces on which she could walk and take her exercise.

The only means of reaching the pavilion from the outside would be by way of the river in a boat. However, T'so Ling felt satisfied that his daughter was safe in prison now, for the windows of his sitting room overlooked Koong-se's apartments and enabled him to keep a close watch on her movements. It would be impossible for a boat to draw near without being seen by the ever-watchful mandarin.

Koong-se was imprisoned indeed. She languished day by day beneath the watchful eyes of the old hag and her ambitious father. Even her little nightingale seemed to sense her sadness, for he sang no more in his golden cage, but hung his head in sorrow.

One day the mandarin entered her rooms beaming and rubbing his hands in a self-satisfied manner. He announced that he had betrothed her to a rich and powerful friend—a Ta-jin, or duke of high

THE TA-JIN

degree. She had never seen the Ta-jin, but as it was customary for parents to arrange such matters, she thought little of that. The news hardly made her unhappier, for in losing Chang she had lost all interest in life.

The wedding was arranged between the mandarin and the Ta-jin. It was to take place in the spring when the peach tree burst into full bloom. The willow was now flowery with blossoms, but the peach tree had scarcely formed its buds.

Koong-se sat on her terrace and sadly watched the humming-birds as they darted through the flowers. She watched the buds of the peach tree as they opened, one by one, Soon, she knew, the peach blossoms would begin to bloom and she would truly be lost to Chang forever.

One morning she felt a spark of hope as her heart was cheered by a good omen. A little bird had started to build its nest in the cornice above her window. She watched for hours as it carried twigs and bits of straw to weave into its little home. Something would surely happen, she thought, for the building of a bird's nest was a sign of good fortune.

THE PAVILION

As dusk was falling she looked out over the water and saw a little boat sailing toward her. It was a toy boat made of a cocoanut shell with a paper sail. The current soon carried the boat close to the shore and she drew it in with her parasol. In it she found a tiny pink pearl wrapped in a piece of bamboo paper. She uttered an exclamation of joy when she saw the pearl, for it was one that she had given to Chang in happier days. She knew then that the boat had been sent by her lover.

Her exclamation brought the old nurse running to see what had happened, but Koong-se hid the little boat in the folds of her robe. As soon as she was alone she examined the piece of paper and found a message written on it. With her heart fluttering like the little bird in the nest, she read: *"As this boat sails to you, so fly all my thoughts. When the willow blossom drops from the bough and folds its buds, your faithful Chang will sink with the lotus bloom beneath the deep waters, leaving only circles on the smooth river like those made by the falling petals. Cast your thoughts upon the waters as I have done and I will hear your words."*

She read the message again and again and then burst into tears at the thought of Chang casting himself into the river. She tore the bottom from the paper on which the message was written and wrote: *"The wise man gathers the fruit he fears will be stolen. The fruit you most prize will be gathered when the peach blossoms burst into bloom."*

She placed the message in the little boat along with a stick of frankincense. Darkness had fallen softly over the river. She lighted the frankincense and pushed the boat with its cargo out upon the stream. She stood there and watched as it drifted away with the current, fearful that the frail craft might sink. It finally disappeared safely into the darkness and she breathed a sigh of relief, for she felt that this was a good omen. She went back to her rooms to rest, happy for the first time since her father had sent Chang away.

Many days passed while she gazed intently over the broad river, but no more little boats drifted her way. As the days went by her hopes dimmed and she began to mistrust her favorable omens. She felt that surely she would see Chang no more. The little bird chirruped from his nest in the eaves, but she sat and watched the river without listening.

Her father came to her one day, bubbling over with good humor. He brought with him a present from the Ta-jin—a large box of rare jewels. The old mandarin told her that she was a most fortunate daughter to be courted by one so powerful and rich. Tears welled into her eyes as she held the jewel box on her lap with no thought of its contents.

"Surely," she thought, "I am doomed. Chang sends no more messages and I shall wed the ugly old Ta-jin."

The mandarin scolded her for moping and told her to cheer up, for the Ta-jin was due to arrive the next day to perform some of the preliminaries for the wedding. He would take food and wine with the father of his betrothed, according to the custom. It would never do for him to find the little Koong-se,

ARRIVAL OF THE TA-JIN

his promised bride, in tears. She must look happy
and proud at the prospect of such a fine husband.
But Koong-se could not find it in her heart to think
pleasantly about the brave Ta-jin.

The next day the great man arrived amid much
shouting and beating of gongs. His servants formed a
long procession as they made their way to the home
of the mandarin. They shouted of the Ta-jin's fame
and of his great achievements in battle. They carried
huge paper lanterns on which were written his many
titles.

The Ta-jin himself rode in a richly carved and
gilded palanquin carried by twelve stalwart bearers,
which showed his rank to be that of viceroy. A great
man indeed.

The mandarin gave him a flattering reception and
his servants sprinkled the visitor with rose petals as
he entered the house.

Koong-se's father and her prospective husband
sat down to a lavish introduction feast which lasted
for many hours. They ate eggs that were a thousand
years old and peacock tongues pickled in lime juice.
There were rare fruits brought from India and

Persia, and delicate slices of octopus, seasoned with strange spices. They drank many "cups of salutation" between them and as the day wore on their merriment increased. The Ta-jin became boisterous and shouted loudly of his exploits on the battlefield. The mandarin applauded enthusiastically after each recital.

In the midst of the festivities a stranger appeared at the door of the banquet room and asked for alms. The mandarin became annoyed at the intrusion and told him to go away. No one knew that the stranger was Chang in the disguise of a beggar. No one paid any attention to him, for the servants were off in another part of the house conducting a celebration of their own.

Chang seized this opportunity to steal to the pavilion of his beloved. Koong-se fell into his arms weeping with joy when she saw him. Chang implored her to flee with him at once, "—for," said he, "the willow blossom already droops upon the bough."

After hurried preparations they departed. She took along the box of jewels, for she was a wise daughter and knew that there was a use for such

THE WILLOW TREE

things. They stole past the reception party without being seen. The Ta-jin, no longer shouting his own praises, was snoring loudly at the table. Even the mandarin had become drowsy and was nodding his head.

Koong-se and Chang ran out of the house, down the marble steps and toward the bridge. Just then the shriveled old nurse discovered what had happened and she raised a hue and cry. The mandarin came to his senses with a start and, looking toward the bridge, saw the fleeing lovers. He jumped to his

feet and shouted loudly for the servants, but there
was no response, for the servants had been feasting
as gaily as their masters. The old mandarin made
after the pair alone, waddling along with great diffi-
culty, for he was not used to such exertion.

This part of the story is shown on the plate by the
three little figures on the bridge. The first is
Koong-se, carrying a distaff, the symbol of girlhood.
Next comes Chang, providently carrying the box of
jewels—and last is the irate father who carries a whip
with which he hopes to chastise the fleeing lovers.

Koong-se and Chang easily outdistanced the tipsy mandarin. They made their way to the home of the faithful nurse, Chun Soy, whom the mandarin had discharged. She lived with her husband who still worked on the mandarin's estate as a gardener. These kind people took the lovers in and witnessed the simple ceremony that made them man and wife.

CHUN SOY

THE GARDENER

They were given a room in the little house which seemed better than a palace to them in their happiness. They spent their days blissfully wandering hand in hand about the cultivated slopes of the hills near their hiding place. At night they looked from their window at the moonbeams dancing on the surface of the river and they breathed the scented air wafted down from the orange groves.

At the home of the mandarin there was a different scene. T'so Ling was beside himself with anger and despair. The Ta-jin bellowed loudly and swore that he had been cheated. He employed spies who searched the countryside for miles around for a trace of the lovers. Using his powers as a magistrate of the district, he issued a proclamation and offered a huge reward for the capture of Chang. He swore that Chang would be put to death for the theft of the jewels. He promised that Koong-se would also be put to death unless she obeyed her father's wishes. There was a great hullabaloo, but never a trace of the fugitives.

Chun Soy's husband, the gardener, kept the newly wedded pair informed of the steps taken to effect their arrest. It was arranged that if suspicion should fall upon their hiding place, he would fail to return at his accustomed time in the evening. Chang and his bride were ready to depart again at any moment, should the spies discover their retreat.

At last the mandarin issued a proclamation declaring that he would forgive his daughter if she would return and forsake her husband. Chang was overjoyed at the thought that the old man should relent at all. He felt that perhaps some day he would forgive his daughter, even though she remained with her husband. He sat on the river bank and composed a song in which he sang of his joy.

While he was singing he was overheard by a passing stranger—a spy in the employ of the Ta-jin. The stranger, feeling that Chang's actions were strange, ran to the home of the mandarin to report his suspicions. The Ta-jin ordered that the poor little house near the bridge be watched.

That evening the gardener failed to return home at his usual time. The lovers made quick preparations and were about to take their departure when Chun Soy came to them with the news that soldiers were stationed in front of the house. The only other way for them to leave was on the river which ran past the back of the house. Now it was turbulent and swollen with the recent rains.

While they were discussing the best course to pursue a loud knock was heard at the door. Chun Soy quickly pulled a screen across the entrance to the lovers' room. Just then a captain of the guard burst into the house and looked about him with suspicion. He read the proclamation of the Ta-jin to Chun Soy in a loud voice and pointed to the great reward that was offered for Chang's capture.

The faithful nurse looked innocent and pretended to be greatly interested in the reward. She asked the captain to read the proclamation again and kept him in conversation for so long a time that at last he began to have his doubts about her. He called in some of his soldiers and told them to search the house. Chun Soy screamed as they entered the room of the young couple. She followed the soldiers in, expecting to find Chang a prisoner and his little bride about to be carried off to the Ta-jin. But the room was empty!

THE CAPTAIN OF THE GUARD

She looked through the window and saw, far out on the swift current, a small boat bobbing about in the waves. She could see Chang standing in the bow and she knew that Koong-se was safe in the deck-house.

The boat was too far away for the soldiers to discover that their birds had flown. They left the house angrily, unable to find either the lovers or anything worth stealing. They searched the near-by rice fields, their tempers getting worse as they plowed through the marshy ground. They had a suspicion that Chun Soy had in some way outwitted them, but she still regarded them innocently and they finally marched away across the bridge.

The boat floated down with the swift current of the river all that night. Chang sat in the prow, silently watching while his little bride slept in the deckhouse. As the first streaks of dawn spread across the sky and silhouetted the distant mountains they drifted into the main river, the Yangtse-Kiang. At times it took great effort and skill on the part of Chang to keep their boat from being smashed to pieces on the rocks.

By the time the sun was up they entered upon more placid waters and they found themselves in the company of numerous other craft, all bent in the same direction. Chang discovered that these boats carried the yearly tribute of salt and rice to the Emperor. He sold one of the jewels to a boatman and from another purchased some food.

For several days they floated along the river toward the sea. As they journeyed onward the river traffic increased. They could tell by the great numbers of houseboats and huge junks that they were approaching a large city. Chang learned from one of the boatmen that all outward bound boats were examined there by the city mandarins.

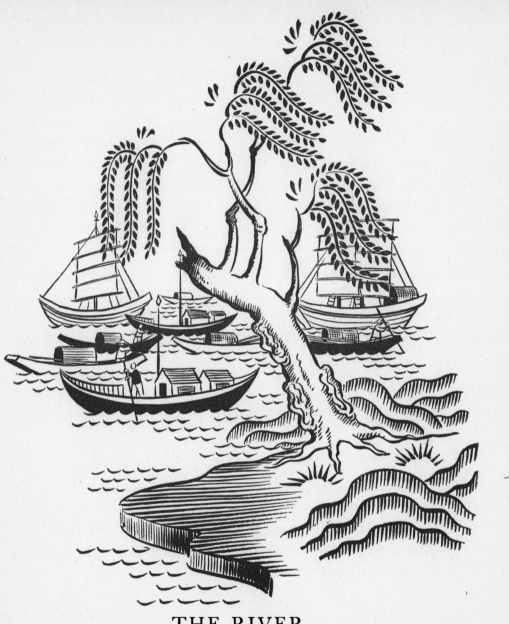

THE RIVER

Chang knew that they would be in danger of dis-
covery if they proceeded toward the city. He moored
the boat on the shores of a little island—a small piece
of ground overgrown with reeds and a few low
shrubs.

Chang and Koong-se liked the island and resolved
to stay there and make the place their home. Here,
they thought, they would be safe.

They sold the rest of the jewels and were able to buy the small piece of ground. They bought tools and set to work, side by side, to create for themselves a home. Together they cultivated the land and set out an orchard of young trees. Koong-se helped with her own hands to build the house. Carefully they tilled every inch of ground on the island. They cared for their gardens well, and they prospered. As the years went by they were able to hire servants to help them. The little island became a paradise of growing things and they were happy.

Now Chang was able to start writing once again, for he had leisure. He wrote a book on agriculture which earned him a great reputation throughout the land. Men came from far and near to observe the results of his experiments in farming, for he had studied to get the most out of his small island.

The book which gained him his reputation, however, also revealed his whereabouts to the Ta-jin, who was still determined upon revenge. He proceeded to the neighborhood of Chang's island and visited the local military mandarin. He swore, by beheading a live rooster with his sword, that Chang

45

had stolen his jewels. He neglected to say that he had given them to Koong-se. With a troop of soldiers he embarked for the island, instructing them to kill Chang without mercy.

When the Ta-jin and his soldiers landed upon the island they were met by Chang and his servants. The soldiers fell upon him, and, although he fought back bravely, he fell mortally wounded. His servants, seeing their master dying, fled in terror.

Koong-se witnessed the death of her husband from the steps of her home. She rushed inside to her rooms as the Ta-jin and his soldiers marched toward her. While they tried to force their way in she set fire to the house and calmly sat down to perish in the flames.

The Ta-jin got little satisfaction from this, however, for the angry gods cursed him with a dreadful calamity and caused him to die friendless and unpitied. There were no children to scatter scented papers over his lonely grave.

But the gods wept for Chang and little Koong-se and would not allow death to part them. They transformed the lovers into two immortal doves to dwell forever in beauty and constancy.

And that is the story written in pictures on the Willow Plate.

THE END

108689

DATE DUE

DEC 21 '79			
OCT 8 6 1983			

```
J
398.2
T
  Thomas, Leslie
  The story on the Willow plate...
```

Ohio Dominican College Library
1216 Sunbury Road
Columbus, Ohio 43219

DEMCO